KITTY CORNER

CALLIE

**Don't miss any of these
stories by Ellen Miles!**

KITTY CORNER

Callie

Otis

THE PUPPY PLACE

Baxter	*Moose*
Bear	*Muttley*
Bella	*Noodle*
Buddy	*Patches*
Chewy and Chica	*Princess*
Cody	*Pugsley*
Flash	*Rascal*
Goldie	*Scout*
Honey	*Shadow*
Jack	*Snowball*
Lucky	*Sweetie*
Maggie and Max	*Ziggy*

CALLIE

ELLEN MILES

SCHOLASTIC INC.

New York   Toronto   London   Auckland
Sydney   Mexico City   New Delhi   Hong Kong

*With special thanks to my
kitty expert Kristin Earhart,
for all her help.*

No part of this publication may be reproduced, stored in a retrieval system, or transmitted in any form or by any means, electronic, mechanical, photocopying, recording, or otherwise, without written permission of the publisher. For information regarding permission, write to Scholastic Inc., Attention: Permissions Department, 557 Broadway, New York, NY 10012.

ISBN 978-0-545-27572-9

Cover art by Mary Ann Lasher
Cover design by Tim Hall

12 11 10 9 8 7 6 5 4 3   11 12 13 14 15 16/0

Printed in the U.S.A.   40

First printing, January 2011

CHAPTER ONE

"Hey, Michael, wait up!" Mia Battelli raced along the sidewalk, trying to catch up with her big brother.

Mia stepped on her scooter brake, slowing down so she could adjust the painting she had rolled under her arm. She glanced up the street to see her brother. As usual, he was way ahead. Michael was always full of energy, even after running back and forth on a basketball court for two hours.

Mia and Michael were heading home from their after-school programs at the community center where their dad worked. Mia was taking art, and Michael played in a basketball league.

"Don't be such a slug bug," Michael yelled over

his shoulder. "We have to hurry if you want to stop at Wags and Whiskers." Hearing that, Mia grabbed her handlebars and pushed off. She always looked forward to seeing the animals on display in the large picture window of the Wags and Whiskers veterinary office. The vet, Dr. Bulford, often kept pets while their owners were out of town. Dr. Bulford also worked with the local animal shelter, trying to find good families for animals who didn't have homes. Sometimes she let Mia and Michael come in and pet the animals in the window.

When Mia saw Michael curve around the corner of the brick building at the end of the block, she pushed her scooter even harder.

A few moments later, Mia rounded the same turn and stopped short in front of Wags and Whiskers. There, nestled between a cage of mixed-breed puppies and one holding a full-grown Siamese cat, were three of the cutest kittens she had ever seen. The kittens blinked and stretched, as if they'd just woken up from a nap.

"Oh!" Mia said. "They're adorable. They must be new. I've never seen them here before." Two of the kittens were tabbies. One had orange and cream stripes, and the other's stripes were gray and white. But the most adorable kitten was black with bright green eyes and a fluffy patch of white under his chin. "Look, it's a tuxedo cat. He looks like he's dressed up in a fancy suit." Mia loved black-and-white cats. "If he were mine, I'd call him Oreo."

"Yuck." Michael made a face. "You should never name a pet after food. You aren't going to eat him, are you?"

Mia made a face back. She hated to admit it, but maybe Michael had a point.

"Besides," Michael continued, "you know Mom won't let us have a pet. And if she ever did, I'd make sure it was a puppy." Michael pointed to a white puppy with a caramel-colored spot around one of his deep brown eyes.

"No way!" Mia said. "If we get a pet, it will definitely be a cat." She couldn't let Michael pick their pet just because he was two years older. Cats were much cooler than dogs. They could curl up on your lap, they didn't need daily walks, and best of all, they could purr. Mia had wanted a cat *forever*. She just *had* to have a cat!

The little puppy Michael liked was cute, but the black kitten was even cuter. A bright pink tongue poked out of the kitten's mouth when he yawned, and Mia could see his tiny—and pointy!—white teeth.

Those teeth reminded her that house cats are related to the great cats who live in the wild. Mia loved to read about lions, jaguars, tigers, and leopards. She did all her school reports on the great cats, including facts about how fast they can run and how far they can leap. The whole bottom row of the bookshelf in her room was filled with animal books.

The black kitten toddled toward the window. "Oh, you are so sweet!" Mia said.

Just then, Dr. Bulford came into the office's front room. She waved when she saw Mia and Michael looking in.

Mia bit her lip. She really wanted to hold one of the kittens. Actually, she wanted to *have* the tuxedo kitten, but she knew Michael was right. Mom was not about to let them have a pet of their own, not in their tiny apartment with its tiny yard. Their mom believed that animals needed a lot of space to explore and grow. She'd had cats and dogs when she was a kid, but she had grown up in the country, in a big house with a big yard.

"Come on. Mom has to leave soon." Michael tugged on Mia's shirt. "Race you to our house!" Michael zoomed off before Mia could even get her painting back under her arm. She glanced back at the kitten and then hurried after her brother, catching up at the corner when Michael had to stop and wait for the traffic light to change. They looked both ways and walked their scooters across the street (a family rule). As soon as they hit the curb, they jumped back on the boards and raced to their house at the next corner. "Tie!" Michael yelled as he skidded to a stop.

Mia and Michael carried their scooters through the gate and up the stoop, the wide steps that led to the front door of their brownstone building. Halfway up, Mia stopped short. "Wait, Michael," she said. "Did you hear that?"

"Hear what?" her brother asked.

Mia paused, trying to listen. "A meow," she whispered. From her spot on the stoop, she looked down at the trash and recycling cans along one side of the building. She searched between her mom's flowers and potted plants. She looked at the tree-lined street and saw cars parked along the curb, people walking dogs, a girl on a bike,

6

and a dad pushing a stroller. She saw a lot of things, but no cat. Where had that meow come from?

"It wasn't anything. You just imagined it," Michael said. "You're so cat-crazy, you can probably still hear the kittens all the way from Wags and Whiskers."

"No, I'm sure I heard a meow," Mia said. "And it sounded sad."

"Come on, Mia." Michael started up the stairs again. "You'll be the sad one if you don't get to see Mom before she has to go to the shop."

Mia took one last look under the stoop and sighed. Michael was right. If she didn't hurry, she would miss Mom. Mia would hate that. Their mom worked at a garden shop a few blocks away. Two nights a week, Julia Battelli went in late, stayed until the store closed, then organized the cut flowers and planting supplies for the next day. She usually didn't get home until after ten, so Dad was in charge on those nights.

Mia stepped inside the building and parked her scooter right next to her brother's under the family coatrack in the hallway. She could hear Michael already talking to their mom in the apartment. Mia had things to tell Mom, too, but before she went in she tiptoed back to the door, placed one hand on its old carved wood, and leaned outside. Aha! There! She saw a flash of color right by the trash can. Was it white, or maybe orange? She couldn't be sure, but she knew she'd seen something.

"Mia!" her mom called. "Mia, where are you?"

Mia hesitated. Then she let the door close. First she would see her mom. Next she would decide what to do about the special something outside. For now, it would be her secret.

CHAPTER TWO

"Mom!" Mia called as she kicked off her purple sneakers and tucked them under the shoe rack in the hallway. She pushed open the door to the apartment. "Mom!"

"In here, Mia."

Mia followed her mother's voice into the kitchen. Mom was crouched down, peeking into the oven. Michael was leaning against the fridge. They had the same thick, dark, wavy hair, but Michael's was cut short and Mom's was pulled back in a ponytail.

They both looked up when Mia walked in. "Hi, sweetheart," Mom said.

"I painted something today." Mia started to

unroll the painting from her art class, a little at a time. "Guess what it is."

"A tiger," Michael said.

Mia knew he would guess that. She loved to paint tigers, but she had done something different this time. "No," she replied. "Not a tiger."

"A leopard?" Mom guessed.

"Close. It has spots," Mia said. She unrolled the painting all the way. "A jaguar! Did you know that jaguars are the third-biggest of the great cats, right after tigers and lions?"

Mom and Michael smiled at each other.

"No, I didn't know, Mia, but I did have a feeling you'd painted some kind of cat. Hmmm . . . I wonder how I guessed that." Mom smiled at her.

Mia wanted to tell her mom about what she had heard and seen outside, but she decided to wait. First she had to find out for herself just what it was. So instead, she added her new painting to the refrigerator door, right next to three of her other great-cat masterpieces.

"Sorry we were late," Michael said. "Mia couldn't stop drooling over the new kittens in the window at Wags and Whiskers."

Mia made a face at her brother. "Oh, and you weren't in love with that puppy?"

"Let's not get into this again," Mom advised as she pulled on an oven mitt. "We all love animals, but we don't exactly have the space around here for another living thing. There's barely enough room for the four of us and a couple of house-plants."

"Yeah, what if we got a pet and it grew as much as the tree in your bedroom?" Michael asked Mom.

"Exactly," Mom answered. They all turned to look through the bedroom doorway at the tall tree, its leafy limbs blocking almost an entire window. "I had no idea that a ficus tree could get so big so fast."

"It's too big," Michael said. "It's going to bust through the ceiling."

"Mom's just really good with plants," Mia said.

"Well, I'd be good with a dog." Michael obviously wasn't ready to drop the subject.

"And I'd be good with a cat," Mia added quickly, putting her hands on her hips.

"That's enough, you two," Mom said with a laugh. "Now, who wants a homemade granola bar?"

"Me!" they both yelled.

"At last, something you can agree on," Mom said. The smell of cinnamon filled the air as she pulled a baking pan from the oven. "Wash your hands and get your books out on the table. The bars will be cool by the time you're ready."

Soon they were all sitting at the long wooden dining room table, where Mia and Michael always did their homework. Mia pulled her math notebook out of her backpack and set it on the table.

"So," Mom began, "your dad will be home in a little while. Mrs. Brennan will stay with you until he gets here."

Mrs. Brennan was their upstairs neighbor. She often watched Mia and Michael after school, even though at eight and ten years old they both thought they were too old for a babysitter.

"If you want free time with your dad later, you need to get all your work done now," Mom reminded them.

"Okay," said Mia. Their mom always liked them to stay at the table and finish their homework all at once. Michael had a hard time sitting still, but Mia usually didn't mind.

That day, however, was different. Mia knew what might be hiding just outside, near the stoop. How could she concentrate on reading about fractions or the Arctic—or on doing any of her other schoolwork—until she found out for sure? She closed her eyes and tried to listen for another sad little meow. But all she heard was the creaking of the old stairs as Mrs. Brennan headed down to their apartment.

In a moment, the door swung open. "Hello?"

"Nonna Kate!" Mia jumped up from the table to greet their neighbor with a big hug.

"Hey, Nonna Kate," Michael said between bites of his granola bar.

Mia knew that Katherine Brennan had lived in the building for over twenty years. She often sat on the front steps and watched the people—and pets—go by. She had been there on the stoop the day the Battelli family had moved in. Mia was the one who had come up with her special nickname. They called her Nonna Kate because "nonna" is Italian for "grandmother."

Nonna Kate's white sneakers squeaked as she came in and took an empty seat at the table.

"Thanks for staying with Mia and Michael today," Mom said.

"Oh, for heaven's sake," said their neighbor. "You know how I love these kids. Any time at all. I'm happy to help."

Mom grabbed her workbag and kissed Mia and Michael good-bye. "Listen to Nonna Kate, kids.

Lay your stuff out for tomorrow, and I'll see you bright and early in the morning." Mia and Michael nodded. They knew the drill on Mom's late nights.

After Mom left, Mia pretended to look at her math notebook again. But really, she was making a plan. It was time to check on the secret something outside. Mia turned a page of her book, tucked in a pencil to hold her place, and scooted back her chair. "I need more water," she said.

Nonna Kate looked up from her newspaper. "I can get it for you, dear," she offered.

"No, thanks. I'll do it." Mia picked up her glass and walked to the kitchen. In a moment, she came back out with a blue recycling bag in her hands. "This is almost full, so I'll just take it out front." Mia walked quickly through the dining room, trying not to look Michael or Nonna Kate in the face.

Mia shoved on her shoes and headed for the front door, the bag in her hands. It wasn't full at all—in fact, it was nearly empty. But it had gotten her outside. She tiptoed down the steps, staring at the area around the trash cans. She didn't see anything, so she tiptoed closer. When Mia was about three steps away, a pink nose and white whiskers appeared from behind the paper-recycling can. A kitten! It really was a kitten! The whiskers disappeared, but then Mia heard that meowing again.

The meows were short and fast. Was the kitten in trouble? "Here, kitty," Mia said. "Here, kitty kitty."

A pretty kitten with bright yellow eyes peeked out from behind the cans. She was a calico, white with splashes of orange and black. She held up one of her front paws and meowed again, showing her pink tongue and white teeth. Mia felt her stomach lurch when she saw the kitten's paw, all swollen and crusted with dried brown blood. Poor thing! No wonder her meow sounded sad, with an injury like that. Mia stayed very, very still. She was dying to get closer, but she didn't want to frighten the kitten away.

Just as Mia was about to reach out her hand—very slowly and carefully—she heard the upstairs door open. "Mia!" Michael called.

The kitten vanished, retreating to her hiding spot behind the cans.

"Mia, what are you doing?" Michael asked from the top of the stoop.

Before Mia could answer, the kitten leapt out from behind the trash can, jumped between the bars of the iron fence, and raced across the sidewalk. Ears back, she bounded under a green car parked in front of the Battellis' building . . . and disappeared.

CHAPTER THREE

"Michael!" Mia yelled. "Did you see her? There *is* a kitten! She was right there." Mia pointed to where she had seen the little calico. "Did you see her before she ran away?"

Michael nodded.

Mia realized that she was yelling. She might be frightening the kitten even more. "She's hurt," she whispered, looking up at her brother. "She has an awful cut on her paw, and she's holding it like this." Mia bent her wrist and let her fingers flop down.

Michael came down the steps. "I knew you were up to something," he said. "You never take out the recycling. That's my chore."

"So?" Mia said. "Now that you scared her off,

are you going to help me find her?" She knelt down on the sidewalk to see if the calico was still under the green car. The kitten was hurt, and she needed Mia.

Michael shook his head. "She's probably long gone by now." He picked up the blue bag and dumped it into the recycling bin.

"Michael, Mia," a voice called from above. Nonna Kate appeared on the stoop. "You aren't supposed to go outside until your homework is done," she reminded them.

"We're not playing." Mia looked up at Nonna Kate. "We saw a kitten, and we're going to rescue her."

"A kitten?" Nonna Kate's voice grew softer for a moment. Then she straightened up and waved her hands. "Oh, no. You are not chasing after stray cats. Not on my watch. You can never be too careful when you're dealing with animals you don't know."

"But the kitten has a terrible cut on her paw."

Mia repeated her injured-cat pose for Nonna Kate. She made her eyes look big and sad, but she could tell that Nonna Kate was not convinced.

"Mia, Michael, back inside." Nonna Kate held the door open. Michael turned and jogged up the steps. Mia stood up, brushed off her hands, and scanned the street one last time.

"Mia." Nonna Kate motioned with her finger.

"All right. I'm coming." Slowly, reluctantly, Mia climbed the steps. She turned around one last time at the top of the stoop, hoping to see the kitten.

"You both need to finish up your lessons." Nonna Kate waved Mia inside and closed the door. "You can discuss the cat with your dad when he gets home."

Mia checked the clock every time she turned a page. She forced her way through her math problems and her Arctic report. If she finished all her work by the time her dad got home, maybe he would let her go back outside to search for the kitten. He would understand that Callie needed their help.

Callie. That was the name Mia had given the calico kitten. Mia sighed whenever she pictured those pretty yellow eyes.

As soon as the clock read 6:20, Mia closed her notebook. "I'm finished. May I get up and wait for Dad?" she asked.

"Of course, dear." Nonna Kate smiled at her. Mia knew that their sitter loved it when she and Michael were polite.

Mia jumped out of her chair and raced to the front bedroom. She pushed her way past the big ficus tree and peered out the window. It was getting dark, but she could make out her dad's springy step at the end of the block. Every second she got a clearer view of his khaki pants, his sneakers, his button-down shirt with the sleeves rolled up, his canvas briefcase, and his friendly smile.

When his foot hit the bottom step of the stoop, Mia knocked on the window and then ran through the apartment to fling open the door.

"No running in the house," Nonna Kate called as Mia dashed by.

"Daddy! Daddy!" Mia greeted her father in the building's hallway, grabbing one of his hands in both of hers. Before Joe Battelli could get through the door, she had blurted out every detail of her afternoon encounter with the sweetest calico kitten ever. "She says, 'Meow, meow, meow,' and she has a horrible cut on her front paw," she told her dad. "We have to find her and help her. We can take care of her until she's better."

"Slow down now, Mia May," her father said, gently brushing her hair behind her ear. "Let me get inside and put down my bag. You can tell me all about it while we make dinner."

Dad pulled off his shoes without untying them. "Hello, Katherine," he said to Nonna Kate. "Thanks so much for staying with the kids."

"You know it's my pleasure." Nonna Kate stood up and gathered her newspaper and magazines.

"No need to rush off," Dad said. "Why don't you stay for spaghetti and meatballs?"

Mia was glad when Nonna Kate thanked Dad but said no. Normally, Mia loved to have company for dinner. But tonight was not a normal night. Tonight, she and Dad and Michael were going to rescue Callie from the street. Mia just knew it.

Between each twirled forkful of spaghetti, Mia talked about Callie. Again and again, she mentioned Callie's sad meow and how she couldn't put weight on her paw. She knew that her dad would eventually give in and agree to find Callie and help her.

"Well, Mia, you know your mom isn't ready for a permanent pet right now." Dad sat back in his chair. "But I guess if we found this kitten and took her in, we'd just be helping a cat in need. We could make sure her paw gets better. What do you think, Michael? You're awfully quiet."

Michael slurped up a strand of pasta and licked his lips. "Well, I didn't really get a good look at her." He swallowed and exchanged glances with Mia. "I feel kind of bad, because she ran off after I opened the door and yelled Mia's name."

"Let's not waste any time feeling bad," said Dad. He wiped his mouth and put down his napkin. "We just need to try to find this kitten." He stood up and started to clear the table.

Mia felt her heart leap. They were going to help Callie! "Her name's Callie," she reminded him.

"That's right. Callie." Dad smiled and ruffled her hair.

Mia and Michael jumped up to help clear away the dishes and Dad searched through the odds-and-ends drawer for the flashlight. Then they all headed out into the night.

CHAPTER FOUR

"Maybe she's under a different car," Mia said hopefully. Mia and Dad had already looked around the trash and recycling cans. Now they were searching under the cars parked in front of their house. Michael stood back and watched the sidewalk and the street. Mia had asked him to do that, in case Callie scampered away without her noticing.

"Okay, let's think about this." Dad put his hand on Mia's shoulder. "She can't be too badly hurt, or else she would still be close by. Maybe the cut on her paw isn't as bad as you think."

Mia wanted to believe her dad, but she still wished they could find the kitten. She headed toward a boxy station wagon and knelt down. "Here, girl," she said softly. "Here, Callie."

"Mia, we've looked under every car." Dad checked his watch. "It's getting late. You and Michael have to go back inside and get ready for bed. Cats are very resourceful—they know how to take care of themselves. I'm sure Callie will be okay."

"But we can't just leave her out here," Mia said. "If she's hurt, she won't be able to catch dinner." Mia knew that stray cats had to hunt for their food, just like the great cats in the wild.

Dad took a deep breath and pushed his hands into his sweatshirt pockets. "How about if we buy some cat food at Mr. Li's? We can put it out by the trash cans. Would that help you feel better?" he asked.

"Yes." Mia gave her dad a small smile.

Dad reached out for Mia's hand and wrapped his other arm around Michael's shoulders as they walked down the street.

Mia liked going to Mr. Li's mini-market. It was

around the corner, in the middle of the block. The tidy, narrow store carried everything from fresh vegetables to boxes of macaroni and cheese to mousetraps, all stacked on floor-to-ceiling shelves. Mr. Li even had fancy ice cream bars in the freezer case by the cash register.

Mr. Li adjusted his wire-rimmed glasses and looked up from his paperwork as they walked into the store. "Hello, hello," he said with a smile. Mia liked the way he always said his greeting twice. "How are you, Battelli family?"

"We're fine," Dad answered with a smile.

"We're going to buy cat food," Mia blurted out. She surprised herself. Somehow, she didn't feel as shy as usual. If she really wanted to help Callie, she needed to speak up.

Mr. Li nodded. "On the back wall. Cans, boxes, and bags."

Mia headed straight to the back of the store and looked at all the fancy-colored labels on the cans: turkey, chicken, salmon, savory stew.

"Let's stick to the dry food, Mia." Dad stepped up behind her.

Mia reached for a giant orange bag.

Dad laughed. "We won't need that much. How about a box?" He pointed to a yellow box and Mia pulled it off the shelf.

"'Kitty Nibbles, meaty mix flavor,'" Mia read to herself as she walked toward the register.

"You got a cat. Congratulations! I like cats," Mr. Li said with an approving nod. He looked right at Mia as he said it.

Mia stared at Mr. Li for a moment. She was buying cat food, so of course he thought she had a cat. But she didn't. She wasn't even close to having a cat of her own.

"Um, not exactly," she began. "There's this cute little calico kitten hanging around near our building. She has a hurt paw, and we want to help her." Mia suddenly felt shy again as she fumbled through her explanation.

"Is she a stray?" Mr. Li asked, his eyebrows raised.

"Yes, we think so," Dad answered, handing a five-dollar bill to the store owner.

"We couldn't find her, but we're going to put food out by our trash cans so she won't be hungry," said Mia.

"It's a good plan," Mr. Li murmured. "I will put out food, too. We will help her together." Mr. Li's lips moved as he counted out the change and placed it in Dad's hand.

"Really?" Mia said hopefully. "Oh, thank you, Mr. Li." She hugged the cat food box close as she, Michael, and Dad headed out the door.

At home, Mia and Michael filled a bowl with food and another with water and put them out near the trash cans. As they climbed the stoop afterward, the night air was cool and still. Mia turned at the door to check the street and sidewalk one last time, but there was no sign of the pretty little kitten. She crossed her fingers and closed her eyes tight, wishing hard that Callie would be there when she woke up in the morning, nibbling at the bowl of food.

CHAPTER FIVE

Mia sat up, rolled out of bed, and raced into her parents' room. Callie had been the first thought in her head that morning, and she was sure that the kitten would be waiting for her by the stoop. She pushed past the ficus tree and the curtains and pressed her face to the window. Looking down, Mia could see that the cat food bowl was empty. But there was no sign of Callie.

"She ate it!" Mia called out. "Callie ate the food. She must be out there!"

Both her parents grumbled. They squinted at her, trying to block out the sun pouring through the open curtain.

"I'm going outside." Mia rushed out of the room.

"No, you are not," Mom called. "Come talk to me first, Mia."

Mia knew that tone. Her mom did not use it often, but it meant business. Mia stopped and frowned. She shuffled back to her parents' room. Her mom was sitting up now.

"Dad told me you saw a stray kitten," Mom said.

Mia nodded. "Her name is Callie," she began. She couldn't wait to tell Mom the whole story. But before she could get going, Mom held up her hand.

"I'm glad you want to help the kitten, Mia," she said, "but I hope you haven't forgotten that we aren't ready for a pet."

Mia nodded.

"I know you want to go outside, but it's a school day. First you have to get ready. Then, if there's time, you can do a quick check around the trash cans before Dad takes you to school." Mom looked

Mia in the eye, and Mia knew there was no point in arguing.

Soon the apartment was full of activity. Dad made coffee, Mom toasted bagels and cut fruit, and Mia and Michael swapped places in the bathroom as they dressed, washed their hands, and brushed their teeth and hair. Mia got so caught up in the flurry of the daily routine that she almost forgot about Callie—until the doorbell rang.

"Who could that be?" Mom asked. Mia fumbled with the strap of her shoe as she watched Mom stride to the door. No one ever came by this early. Mia felt her heart start to beat faster. She forced her heel into her other shoe, grabbed her backpack, and followed Mom out of the apartment and into the hallway. She could see someone through the lace curtains on the building door as Mom started to open it.

"Hello, Mr. Li," Mom said. "How are you this morning?"

Mr. Li? Mia's heart leapt.

"Good. It's a good morning," Mr. Li said.

"Oh, you have the kitten." Mom sounded a little surprised.

The kitten! Mia dropped her backpack and pushed her way past the partly opened door so she was standing next to Mom. She looked up at Mr. Li and saw the little calico kitten cradled in his arms. Mr. Li had found Callie! A buzz of excitement filled Mia's ears. Mom and Mr. Li were talking, but Mia didn't pay attention. She just stared at the kitten. The calico looked small in Mr. Li's arms. She kept moving around, and Mia could see that Mr. Li had to hold on tight so the kitten wouldn't jump down.

Mia felt Mom's hand on her shoulder. "Yes, Mia was very worried about the kitten. She thought there was a cut on her leg. Right, Mia?"

Mia pulled her gaze away from the kitten to look up at her mom. She nodded. "On her paw," she said. Then she turned back to Mr. Li and Callie.

"The cut looks painful. A vet should check it, I think," Mr. Li said. He started to hand Callie to Mom. The kitten's legs dangled in the air, and Mia could see her little curled claws poking out of three pink-padded paws. The cut paw was still brown with blood.

Mom reached out to take the kitten. Mia watched as Mom placed one hand under Callie's chest and cradled her hindquarters in the other. Callie instantly cuddled against Mom.

"Yes, we'll take her to the vet," Mom said to Mr. Li. "We'll let you know how she is. Thank you for bringing her to us."

"Yes, yes." Mr. Li gave a slight bow. He smiled down at Mia, then walked down the stairs and toward his store.

By then, Dad and Michael had come to the door.

"Oh, she's cute," Dad said, reaching out to pet the kitten.

"And wiggly," Mom added, tightening her grip on Callie.

Everyone stared at the little kitten as Mom reported what Mr. Li had told her: He had put food just outside the market door when he'd left at night, and Callie was sitting next to the bowl when he came back in the morning. Callie had stayed with him inside the market until he was able to take a break and bring her to the Battellis' house. "Mia was right," she finished. "She does have a cut on one of her front paws. It looks kind of deep." When Mom gave the hurt paw a gentle squeeze, Callie mewed and pulled it away.

"We have to take her to the vet," Mia said. "Dr. Bulford will know what to do. We should call her right now."

"*We* have to get two kids off to school right now," Mom corrected her. "I'll call Dr. Bulford after you all leave and make an appointment for right after you get out of school, so we can all go together."

Mia frowned. Why did she have to go to school today? She wanted to stay with Callie and play with her. She wanted to take her to the vet right away. She wanted to stamp her feet and shout out, *Callie needs me!* But she knew what Mom would say: Acting out was not the way to get what you wanted. Mia took a deep breath. At least Callie was safe at their house for now. And after school, they would take her to Dr. Bulford's.

"Can I at least hold her first?" Mia asked.

Mom hesitated. "Okay, but just for a minute. You don't want to be late."

Mom held out the kitten, and Mia cradled her carefully. Callie's colorful coat was soft, and she felt small under all that fur. She hardly weighed a thing. "Hey, Callie," Mia said gently. "We looked everywhere for you." The kitten gave three quick meows as she glanced around the hallway, her golden eyes big and bright.

"Are you scared? Don't worry. We're going to take good care of you. We'll make sure you get all better." Mia stroked the kitten under her chin, and Callie closed her eyes and started to purr. Mia could see her nostrils twitch as she sniffed. What did the kitten smell? What was she thinking?

Where am I? This is a new place. It looks new, and it smells new. And there are so many people! I like people, and I love to be petted. This girl is good at petting. But right now I want to investigate this place. I like to know where I am. I like to be in charge of me.

The kitten wiggled around in Mia's arms.

"Okay," Mom said. "It's time for you all to leave and for me to figure out just what we're going to do with this cute and squirmy little cat. I guess I'll have to go down to Mr. Li's and get a litter box, for one thing." She took Callie away from Mia, trading the kitten for a purple backpack.

"Okay, Mia," Dad said. "Let's go." Mia felt his hand on her back, directing her to the door. Michael was already waiting at the bottom of the stoop. Just as she was about to take a step down, Mia whirled around.

"Good-bye, Callie," Mia called. "You be good for Mom, and I'll see you after school. I promise."

Callie stopped fidgeting and looked right at Mia with her bright yellow eyes. Mia was certain the kitten understood: A promise was a promise.

CHAPTER SIX

All day at school Mia watched the hands on the big round clock above her classroom door. It felt like weeks before she was racing out the school's double doors to search for her mom on the corner where they usually met.

When she first spotted Mom, Mia couldn't see Callie. Mia had been picturing Mom holding the kitten in her arms, the way she had at home. Where was that calico kitten? Weren't they taking her to the vet? Then, when she looked closer, Mia noticed a cloth pet carrier strapped across Mom's shoulder. Mia leapt down the stairs, pushed her way through the crowd of kids, and raced up to Mom.

"Hi, Mom." Mia bent down to see through the

mesh windows of the carrier. "Hi, Callie." The kitten was huddled in the back corner of the carrier. Mom had put an old towel in there with her, but Callie still looked cold and scared.

"I borrowed the carrier from Nonna Kate. It's from when she had a cat. But I don't think Callie likes it in there," Mom said. "I don't think she likes being closed in, period. She kept trying to sneak outside all day long."

Mia was glad that Callie hadn't escaped. The kitten shouldn't be running around outside with that nasty cut.

"Oh, is that your cat, Mia? She's adorable."

Mia looked up to see Carmen, a girl in her class, standing beside her. Carmen had never really talked to her before.

"I just love calicoes," Carmen said. "Did you know that almost all calicoes are girls? Only like one in three thousand is a boy. Weird, huh?" She bent over to get a closer look at Callie.

Mia was surprised. Carmen knew about cats?

"Well, she's not exactly *our* cat," Mia said.

Carmen stood up and gave Mia a long look. She lifted her wavy black hair over her shoulder. "What do you mean?"

"We're just taking care of this kitten," Mom said. "Mia helped rescue her from the street. Her foot is cut, and we're taking her to the vet."

"Cool," Carmen said. She twirled a guitar key chain on her finger. "You're lucky. My mom won't let us have a cat. Too much hair."

"Yeah," Mia said with a sigh. "But we're just keeping her for a while, until her foot is better. Then maybe we'll help find her a home."

"Well, fostering a cat is better than nothing," Carmen said. "I still say you're lucky. See you, Mia." She gave a quick wave and walked away.

Fostering. Mia liked the sound of that. It was better than just having Callie "visit." After Carmen was out of earshot, Mia looked up at her mom. "How long can we foster Callie?"

Mom didn't answer. Instead, she said, "Here

comes Michael." She motioned to Michael to meet them farther up the sidewalk, and gave Mia a gentle nudge. Mia tried to bend down as she walked so she could see Callie. As soon as Mom started to move, Callie started to meow.

Oh, no. Here we go again. I don't like this feeling. I can hardly stand up! And there's no way out of this bag. I'm glad to see the girl again. She has a kind voice. Maybe she will let me out.

"It's okay, Callie. We'll be at Wags and Whiskers soon." Mia tried to reassure the kitten, whose eyes were wide with fright. "You're going to love Dr. Bulford. She'll help you get all better."

Soon they were sitting in the Wags and Whiskers waiting room. Mia had often stared at the pet owners through the front window, wishing she had a pet, too. But now she was just worried about Callie. The kitten held up her hurt paw and licked it.

43

Dr. Bulford appeared behind the reception desk, her strawberry blond hair shoved behind her ears. "Callie?" she called, glancing around the room. Mia saw the vet smile when she, Mom, and Michael stood up. "Follow me," Dr. Bulford said as she headed down a long hallway.

Once they were in the examination room, Mom shook Dr. Bulford's hand and introduced everyone.

"Oh, I've met Mia and Michael. They're real animal lovers," Dr. Bulford said. Her voice was warm and kind. "I'm so glad your family has adopted a kitten." She put her hand on the carrier.

"But we haven't," Mia said.

The vet looked confused.

"Callie turned up on our block yesterday," Mom explained. "We took her in because she has a cut on her paw. We thought she needed some medical attention."

"I named her Callie because she's a—" Mia began.

"Calico," Dr. Bulford said, smiling and nodding. "Cute. Well, since Callie's a stray, I'll have to give her a full exam to make sure she's healthy. But let's have a look at that paw first."

Mom unzipped the bag and Callie poked her head out, her paws resting on the top of the carrier.

Finally. We stopped moving. And the bag is open. I'll peek around first, and then I'll explore!

When Callie peeked out of the carrier, Mia thought she looked just like a picture in a cat calendar. Adorable. Then Callie sneezed, and she looked even cuter. Michael laughed. He smiled at Mia. "She's pretty funny for a cat," he said.

With a mighty leap, Callie burst out of the carrier and landed on Dr. Bulford's examination table. "You're a frisky one, aren't you?" the vet said. "I won't hurt you. I just need to look at that paw." She reached for Callie, but the kitten jumped off the table and onto the floor. She ran to hide under a chair.

Dr. Bulford laughed. "Guess that cut doesn't slow her down much." She was obviously used to animals trying to hide. In no time, she had picked Callie up and was investigating the cut. Callie let out a low growl, and her body seemed to stiffen. Mia winced. She hoped it didn't hurt too much. Michael reached out to squeeze Mia's hand. She squeezed back.

"It's okay, girl," the vet said, reassuring Callie. She clucked her tongue and scratched the kitten under the chin before looking up at Mia and her family. "You did the right thing, bringing her in," Dr. Bulford said. "Her foot would probably heal fine on its own, but just in case I'll put in a few stitches and give her some medicine to stop any infection." She paused. "We also need to talk about the fact that she's a stray."

Mom looked at Mia and Michael. Mia squeezed Michael's hand again.

"I get the feeling from my exam that Callie has been on the streets for a while, so I'm guessing she does not have a family of her own," Dr. Bulford said. "Are you willing to give her a home once she's better?"

Mia wanted to yell out, *Yes, yes, yes!* She was dying to give Callie a home, but she knew it wasn't up to her to decide. She looked at Mom.

"We're really not ready to adopt a kitten permanently," Mom said.

The vet nodded.

Dr. Bulford tilted her head to one side as she continued to examine Callie. "Now that I think of it, she looks familiar," the vet said. "I think I've seen her prowling along Park Street over the past few months." The vet looked into the kitten's ears and mouth, and stroked Callie's fur. She started right between the ears and ran her hand all the way down Callie's back. "She seems healthy, but I don't recommend letting cats live outside in this neighborhood. It's too busy."

"Callie has a hard time staying indoors," Mom said. She fiddled with the carrier strap. "All day she either stared out the window or stalked near the door, just waiting for a chance to get out."

"As a vet, I can't advise you to let her back on the streets," said Dr. Bulford. "But I know there are some cats who just can't live inside." She gathered Callie into her arms. "I'll need to take her in the back to stitch up her paw. You can wait in the reception area. Don't worry, we'll take good care of her. In the meantime, I need you to make a big decision. Is Callie going to heal here at the clinic, or will she be going home with you?"

Mia caught her breath. She looked at Michael, and they both looked at Mom. Mia crossed her fingers.

CHAPTER SEVEN

"Please, Mom," Mia said in her sweetest voice, out in the waiting room. "Callie needs us." She didn't say any more. Mom *hated* begging.

"Just give me a minute," Mom replied. "I'm thinking."

"I'll help," Michael said. "I mean, Mia and I will take care of her."

Mom turned and studied Michael. "Really?" she asked.

"Sure," he replied.

Mia stared at Michael. She had never expected him to want to help with Callie. Michael looked past Mom and his eyes met Mia's. He shrugged and smiled. "She's not a dog, but she's okay," he said.

"All right," Mom said. "We can take her with us. But just until she gets better. Then we'll have to find a real home for her."

Mia wanted to jump for joy. They were taking Callie back home!

When Dr. Bulford brought Callie out to the waiting room, Mia listened closely to everything the vet said. She told the Battellis to bring Callie back to the office in one week so she could look at the wound. By then, the stitches would have dissolved. "Meanwhile, you need to keep Callie inside so she can heal properly," the vet finished. "That cut has to stay clean so it won't become infected." She smiled at Mia. "Have fun with Callie," she said. "She's lucky to have you to take care of her."

As they left Wags and Whiskers, Mom mentioned that she needed some vegetables for dinner that night. Mia skipped all the way to Mr. Li's market. A week! She had a whole week with Callie. That had to be enough time to convince Mom to keep Callie forever — especially if Michael helped.

"I'll wait out here with Callie," Mom said when they got to the market. "You two go in and get a bell pepper and a bunch of broccoli." Mom handed Michael some money. Mia waved to Callie and then followed her brother inside.

When they went up to the cash register, Mia was too excited to be shy. Quickly, she told Mr. Li all about what had happened at the vet and how Mom had agreed that they could take Callie home while she healed. Mr. Li listened closely as he made change and put their vegetables in a bag.

"Where is Callie now?" he asked.

"She's right outside with Mom," Mia said.

Mr. Li glanced around the store to make sure no one was ready to check out. Then he walked out from behind the register, past the waist-high freezer case and the gum and candy shelves, and through the door.

"Oh, hello, Mr. Li," Mom said. "I'll bet you want to say hi to Callie. She's doing well, thanks to you."

Mr. Li stooped down so he could look through the carrier window. "Hello, hello, little kitty," he cooed. He scratched at the carrier with his index finger. Callie meowed through the mesh.

It's my friend from the store. I can still smell that yummy food he gave me. Fish. Delicious. And I remember how he scratched me under the chin. I like to be petted there.

Mr. Li smiled. "Remember me? I was lonely after you left. Come visit me anytime. I'm glad you are feeling better."

Mia knew how Mr. Li felt. She had felt lonely at school, too. She had spent the whole day thinking about Callie.

Mia laughed. Now Callie was trying to paw at Mr. Li from inside the carrier.

"She's waving at you," Michael said.

Mr. Li smiled at Callie. "I need to get back," he said, pointing at the store.

"Come on," Mia said, after Mr. Li had disappeared back into his market. She couldn't wait to get home. She wanted to hold Callie, play with Callie, and just watch Callie walk around their apartment.

At home, Mia and Michael raced through their homework, then played with Callie while Mom worked in the kitchen. They pulled a string and Callie chased it. The excited kitten scampered after the twine, batting at it with her claws extended. Mia loved how Callie's ears twitched just before she was about to pounce. When she was playing, her paw didn't seem to hurt one bit.

Michael dragged the string into his room and climbed up on the bed. Mia watched as the string slithered behind him. Callie watched, too. The kitten hunched down. She held her head close to the floor and twitched her tail in the air. Then Callie tore across the room and sprang up on the bed, her teeth and claws tearing at the quilt. Michael and Mia cracked up.

Dad got home just before dinner was ready. "We're in here," Michael called. "With Callie."

Mia looked up when Dad appeared in the doorway. She was holding Callie in her lap, and she could feel the kitten's gentle, even purr each time she stroked the white fur on her neck.

Dad bent down and scratched the kitten behind the ears. "Hi there, Miss Callie. Aren't you a happy cat?" Callie purred even louder.

Oh, I could get used to this! These people know how to play and how to pet. I'll rest for another minute; then I'll look around some more.

Dinner conversation was all Callie, Callie, and more Callie. While they ate and talked, Mia watched Callie. The kitten sat on the sill of Mom and Dad's bedroom window and stared outside, peering around the branches of the ficus tree.

"Can Callie sleep at the bottom of my bed?" Mia asked.

"Not tonight, honey," Mom said. "She may want to explore in the middle of the night, and I wouldn't want her to keep you up. We'll make her a little bed in the family room."

Mia nodded and looked down at her food. Mom was right. Mia knew that the great cats were nocturnal and did most of their hunting between sunset and sunrise, so Callie might be up late. Still, Mia was disappointed. She had always dreamed of having a cat sleep on her bed, keeping her feet warm.

While Mia was in the bathtub, she heard Mom open the linen closet, searching for some old towels for Callie to sleep on. She could also hear Dad and Michael taking out the trash. She thought about how, just the night before, they had searched for Callie around the trash cans and under the cars. Now Callie was safe inside with them.

After her bath, Mia got into her pajamas and went to inspect the cat bed Mom had put in a spot next to the couch. It was a soft pile of towels topped with one of Mia's old baby blankets. Mia knew that Callie would love it.

"Let's show it to her," Mia said to Mom.

"Okay. I think she's in the front window," Mom said. "Be gentle when you pick her up. Watch out for her paw."

Mia rushed into her parents' room, but Callie wasn't there. She looked on all the windowsills, behind the big plant, and under the bed.

"Mom, she's not here!" Mia yelled. She looked around the room again and then headed back to the family room.

Mom came from the back of the apartment. "She wasn't in your or Michael's room, either," Mom said.

When Dad and Michael came back from taking out the trash, Dad looked first at Mom, then at Mia. "What's wrong?" he asked.

Mia didn't even want to say the words. Mom put a hand on her shoulder. "Callie's gone," she said.

CHAPTER EIGHT

Mia and Michael and Mom searched every nook and cranny of the apartment while Dad headed back outside to look for Callie. "Any luck?" Mom asked when Dad came in again.

Dad shook his head. "I checked with Nonna Kate, too. Callie isn't up there. Maybe she slipped out when we were taking out the trash. I just don't know how she did it."

"We were really careful," Michael told Mia.

Mia couldn't believe it. Callie was gone. When she looked at the empty cat bed, she felt a single tear roll down the side of her nose.

"We can look for her some more," Dad said. "And we'll put food out."

Mom and Michael started filling up Callie's

bowls while Dad helped Mia with her coat and shoes. She put them on right over her pajamas.

"We'll be back!" Dad called as they opened the door.

Mom ran down the hall to give Mia a small Tupperware bowl. The container had a lid and was filled with Callie's food.

"If you shake it, she might hear the rattling and come," Dad said.

At first, Mia just held the container. She tip-toed along the sidewalk and whispered Callie's name into the dark night. Every time a car drove past, Mia flinched. She remembered that Dr. Bulford had said it wasn't a good idea for cats to live outside in a busy neighborhood. By the time they got to the end of the street, Mia was shaking the bowl and calling as loudly as she could. Dad held her hand, giving it a squeeze every once in a while.

Once they came around to Park Street, Mia had pretty much given up hope. At the next corner, they would have walked all the way around the block.

"Mr. Li!" Mia cried. The light was still on in his store. Mia let go of Dad's hand and ran down the street to the market door. The store was closed, but Mia could see Mr. Li inside. He was sweeping in the back. Mia banged on the glass door. "Mr. Li!" she yelled.

"Mia!" Dad called. "Don't bother Mr. Li."

It was too late. Mr. Li had already propped the broom against the shelves and was coming toward the front of the store. Mia held her breath as he turned the locks.

"Hello, hello," Mr. Li said as he pulled the door open. "Is everything all right?" His faced was creased with worry.

Dad caught up and put his hand on Mia's shoulder. "We're sorry to bug you—"

"Callie's gone," Mia interrupted. "She must have gotten outside. We can't find her, and the vet told us to keep her inside until her cut is better."

"Ah, yes," Mr. Li said, his eyebrows raised. "Cats do that. Callie is like my old cat. She *hated* closed doors. She wanted to come and go, so I kept the store door open. Then she didn't leave. She just wanted to be able to go. Funny old cat." Mr. Li shook his head and smiled. Then he looked at Mia as if he had just remembered she was there. "I will leave food out again. Your cat will be hungry. She will come back. You leave out food, too."

Mr. Li's words made Mia feel better. He seemed so sure Callie was not lost. She nodded and gave the store owner a small smile.

"Thank you, Mr. Li," said Dad. He took Mia's hand and led her away from the market and down the street. When they got home, Mia stopped at the trash cans. She wanted to make sure Mom and Michael had put Callie's bowls in the right place. She also checked that the kitten was not hiding by the stoop.

Inside, she went straight to bed. Mom and Dad

came in together to tuck her in. They usually took turns, but Mia knew they both felt bad about what had happened. Dad brushed the hair from her forehead. "We'll keep our window open tonight so we can hear her," he promised, "just in case."

"Thanks, Dad," Mia said.

Mom kissed her on the forehead and tugged on her ear. "Love you, Mia. Sweet dreams."

Mia kissed Mom back without answering. How could she have sweet dreams when Callie was lost?

CHAPTER NINE

Mia woke up the next morning and tiptoed into her parents' room. This time, she was careful not to wake them. Pulling back the curtain, Mia could see that the dish was empty. Once again, the food they had left out had disappeared. And once again, Callie was nowhere in sight.

Mia wandered back to her bedroom. She knew that the empty dish was a good sign. If Callie had eaten the food, she was still okay. But Mia wished Callie were inside their house. She really wanted her to stay. She liked Callie's bright yellow eyes and the way she pawed at the window. She liked Callie's little greeting of *meow, meow, meow.*

Mia heard Michael and her parents wake up

and start to move around the apartment. Michael knocked twice and poked his head past her door.

"Any sign of Callie?" he asked.

Mia frowned and shook her head. She saw Michael's face fall. "She did eat the food, though. Thanks for putting it out."

A little later, Mia was brushing her teeth when she heard the phone ring.

"That was Mr. Li," Mom said when Mia came out of the bathroom. "Callie is at his store. She was there when he showed up this morning. Want to come with me to get her?"

Mia was dressed and ready in seconds. Outside, she dashed ahead of Mom and stopped in front of Mr. Li's, out of breath from running so fast. She looked through the window. There was Callie! The kitten looped herself around the legs of a woman buying coffee and toilet paper. The woman bent down to give her a pat. Then a teenager strode in and headed for the potato chip display. Callie trotted down the aisle after him, batting at the boy's loose shoelace. Mia smiled and pushed open the door.

"Hello, hello!" Mr. Li said with a wave. "Your cat is here. She is keeping busy."

Mia rushed down the aisle and swooped the kitten into her arms.

Oh, it's my friend! What's she doing here? I hope she wants to play.

Mia snuggled her nose into Callie's soft belly. She was so happy to see the kitten again. When she looked up, she saw her mom talking to Mr. Li. Mia walked toward them, petting Callie all the way. The kitten purred and rubbed her cheek against Mia's.

"Thanks again, Mr. Li," Mom said.

"Thank you," Mia said, looking Mr. Li right in the eye so he would know how much she appreciated his help.

"My pleasure," he said. "She's a good cat."

Mia was on the sidewalk before she heard Mr. Li calling to her. "Wait!" he said. "I have something for Callie." He came out from behind the register and hurried toward Mia. He held something fuzzy and pink in his hand. "She likes it," he said. "She likes to play."

It was a mouse toy. "Thank you," Mia said. Mr. Li really seemed to understand cats.

Leaving for school was hard. Callie had just gotten home, and Mia was worried she would try to escape again.

"I'll keep a close eye on her," Mom promised. "And I'll call Dr. Bulford to tell her that Callie got out, and ask if she has any ideas on how to deal with a disappearing cat."

Mia rubbed Callie between the ears one last time and kissed her good-bye. Michael waited for her to close the apartment door before he opened the one that led to the street. They had to make sure Callie wouldn't get out again.

Mia tried to pay attention at school, but the day went by in a blur. All she could think about was Callie. As soon as the last bell rang, she and Michael raced the whole way home on their scooters. Mia was relieved to see Callie sitting in the window. The kitten looked like a princess in a castle tower, watching all that went on outside. "Hi, Callie!" Mia said as she climbed the stairs. The kitten blinked at her, then jumped down from the window as soon as Michael put the key in the lock.

Mia parked her scooter and took off her shoes. As usual when they came home, she was a step behind her brother. The instant Michael opened the apartment door, Mia saw a blur of white and orange as Callie zipped out into the hallway. "Oh, no!" said Mia. But the kitten stopped short when she saw that the outside door was closed. She meowed, and Mia could just imagine what she was thinking.

I'm going out! Oh, why is that big door closed? I'll just wait for it to open again. I want to smell the fresh air. I want to hear what's happening outside. I need to know what's going on. Why can't I go out? I'm pretty clever. I'll find a way.

Mom appeared, a dish towel in her hand. "She's been like that all day," she said, sighing. "Whenever she hears someone in the hallway, she searches for an escape route. Callie really wants to get outside. I'm afraid to open any doors or windows when I'm here by myself." She frowned. "We're going to have a family chat at dinner."

Mia gulped. She usually liked family chats. They were times to discuss things together, and everyone got a chance to talk. But this time, Mia knew that the chat could be about only one thing: What would they do with Callie?

Mia tried to put her worries out of her head as she hurried to catch Callie. The kitten was sitting on the entry rug, innocent as could be. "Why are you causing so much trouble?" Mia asked. She and Michael played with Callie until dinner was ready. Even as she giggled at the kitten's antics, Mia worried. How much longer would Callie be with them?

Mom looked very serious when they sat down to dinner. Mia's stomach was in a knot, and even though eggplant parmesan was one of her favorites, she couldn't eat a bite.

"Well, I spoke to Dr. Bulford today," Mom said finally. "I told her how Callie keeps trying to get out, and how I think it's too hard on us and on her to try to keep her inside."

Mia looked at Mom. "But she has to stay indoors until her foot heals," she said.

Mom nodded. "Yes, and Dr. Bulford says she's willing to have her stay at Wags and Whiskers. I think that might be a better place for her."

Mia jumped up from her chair. "She can't stay there! She would hate being in a cage in the window."

Dad put his hand on Mia's shoulder. "Easy, Mia May," he said. "Are there any other choices for Callie?" he asked Mom.

"Well, Mia is probably right," said Mom. "Maybe it would be cruel to put Callie in a cage. Dr. Bulford also said she would be working hard to find a home for Callie, maybe a place with a bigger yard."

Mia just shook her head, feeling tears come to her eyes. If anyone was going to find a home for Callie, it should be her. She knew Callie best.

Mom was still talking. "The only other possibility I can think of is just to let her go back to her old life. Callie is used to being a stray, and maybe it suits her best. She's just not happy being cooped up with us. I told the vet that her paw is healing well, and Dr. Bulford said she would probably manage all right if she escaped. The stitches will dissolve within a few days."

Mia hated the thought of Callie leaving their home. She was just getting used to having a cat around, and she loved it as much as she'd always known she would. And she hated the idea of Callie living her life as a stray. Wouldn't every cat rather have a home and family?

"Callie hates being locked inside, but she really does like people," said Michael, as if he were reading Mia's mind. "She keeps running away, but she always comes back—at least, she goes back to Mr. Li's market."

The whole family looked into the front bedroom. Callie sat in the window, pawing at the glass.

Look at those birds strut along the sidewalk. If I were out there, I'd show them who's the boss. Why is this window closed? I want to get out!

Mia sighed. Why couldn't Callie just be happy

to be inside? What did you do with a cat that loved people but couldn't be cooped up? There didn't seem to be any good answer. Unless . . . "I think I have an idea!" she said.

CHAPTER TEN

"Remember how Mr. Li told us he used to have a cat who liked to get out?" Mia looked around at her family. "And then, when he left the market door open, she pretty much stayed in the store? I wonder if Callie would do the same thing."

"Are you saying what I think you're saying?" asked Dad.

Michael stared at Mia, a slow smile spreading across his face. He nodded. "I know you think I don't like cats," he said, "but Callie kind of changed my mind. I really like her. I wish she could be our pet. But since she can't be ours, it would be great if she belonged to someone we knew, wouldn't it?"

Mia smiled back at her brother. "Someone

who would take good care of her and give her fluffy pink mouse toys," she agreed. "She'd like that."

"And how cool would it be if we could still see her all the time?" Michael added, his eyes sparkling.

"Yeah, that would be the best," Mia agreed. She was getting excited, too. She wondered if it could work. Would Callie be happy? Would she remember Mia and Michael?

A few minutes later, the whole family walked down to Mr. Li's store. Dad and Michael waited outside with Callie in the cat carrier while Mia went in to talk to Mr. Li, with Mom following behind.

Her shyness forgotten, Mia marched right up to the register where the shopkeeper stood, adding up the receipts from the day. "Mr. Li?" she said. "How come you don't have a cat? I mean, would you want another one?"

"Ah, me?" Mr. Li asked. "I like cats very much.

I miss my old cat." He paused. It seemed like he was looking at something far away. "Yes, I would have another cat."

Mia took a couple of deep breaths. "What about Callie? Would you take her?" she asked. "You could just try it out for a while first. And then, if everything went well, maybe you could be her family and your store could be her home."

Mia felt Mom's hand on her shoulder.

"But I thought you were keeping Callie," said Mr. Li.

Mia wished that were true, but she knew it had never been the plan. "We were just fostering her," Mia told him. "Just keeping her until we could find the right home." She felt Mom squeeze her shoulder, and she knew that her mother was proud of her.

Mr. Li began to nod slowly. He raised his eyebrows and his nod quickened. He smiled. "Yes, yes," he said. "I will take her, then. If she is mine, I promise to take good care of her."

"Wait right here," Mia said. She heard Mom start to tell Mr. Li about Callie's paw, and how she would need to see Dr. Bulford one more time. She knew that her mother would take care of all the details. Mia wanted to take care of Callie.

Mia brought the carrier into the store and unzipped the top. Eagerly, Callie jumped out of the carrier. She trotted up and down the main aisle of the narrow little market. Then she walked toward the register, looked up at Mr. Li, and greeted him with a happy *meow, meow!*

"Hello, hello to you, too," he said with a laugh.

Callie rubbed herself against Mr. Li's ankles and meowed some more.

Oh, I like this place. There are so many smells and so many people. There's a lot for me to do. The door is open, so I can always go outside. But for now, I want to watch the door to see who is coming in. Yes, that's what I'll do.

Callie walked over to the front of the market and sat upright, her tail curled about her just so and her eyes on the door. Mia had a feeling that Callie had chosen her spot. It was perfect for her. She was safely inside, not out on the streets. But she was in the middle of the action, where she could watch people come and go. Now Mia knew where to look for the calico kitten whenever she went to Mr. Li's. She and Michael knelt by Callie and gave her some good-bye pets while Mom and Dad talked with Mr. Li.

When Mia and Michael were done playing with Callie, Mr. Li gave them each an ice cream bar. "Thank you for Callie," he said. "Come and see her anytime. Come soon."

On the walk home, Nonna Kate's cat carrier felt light—and empty—in Mia's arms. When they got to their building, they all sat down on their stoop; Mom and Dad sat on the top step, then Michael, then Mia below them all. Mia put the cat carrier down. She still wished Callie were staying with them, but at least she would get to see and play with the calico kitten every day at Mr. Li's.

"Well, that was a busy few days," Mom said.

"Sure was," Dad agreed. "It'll be good to have some peace and quiet."

Mia looked at Michael and rolled her eyes. "I don't want peace or quiet," she said. "I just want to foster another cat."

"Yeah, let's foster lots more cats and kittens — until we're ready for one of our own," Michael said.

Mom and Dad exchanged glances.

"We already have the litter box and the food," Mia said. She could tell by the way her parents had looked at each other that this was a good time to push for what she wanted.

"She has a point. You have to admit, you became very fond of Callie," Dad said, patting Mom on the hand. Mom nodded.

"And fostering is a good thing, right?" Michael said.

"You're right," Mom said. "It is."

"I suppose it would help the kids learn what it takes to have a pet of their own," Dad added. "They were pretty responsible when it came to taking care of Callie."

"Okay, okay, I get it," Mom said. "Let's just wait and see."

"Yes," said Mia. She smiled up at her mom and dad and brother. "Let's just wait and see what kind of kitten we foster next."

KITTY CORNER CAT QUIZ

Callie is a calico cat. Her coat is mostly white, with splotches—or blocks—of orange and black. Calico is her color pattern, but what breed of cat is she?

A. Domestic shorthair

 ### B. Manx

C. Siamese

D. Japanese bobtail

Turn the page for the answer.

The answer is A. Callie is a domestic short-hair. The domestic shorthair is a mixed-breed cat. Domestic shorthair cats come in more than eighty different colors and patterns, including calico, tabby (striped), and solid. Because they are a mix of many breeds, shorthairs come in different shapes and sizes, too. Some are long and lean, while others have a stocky build. The one thing they all have in common is their short, sleek coat.

There are not nearly as many breeds of cats as there are of dogs. Some pure breeds you might have heard of are Siamese, Manx, Maine coon, and Persian.

Cats that are the same breed always share at least one special feature. For example, all Siamese are "pointed" cats, which means that their faces, ears, feet, and tails are darker than the rest of their coats. You can tell Persians by their stocky builds, flat noses, and long, full coats. Huge, long-haired Maine coon cats have extra-big paws for walking through snow (some even have extra toes). And Manx cats have no tails!

Just like dogs, though, every cat has his or her own personality, no matter the breed or mix. That's why we love our cats so much—and why they're so much fun to live with!

KITTY CORNER

Who will be the next kitten in need of a home?

Find out in this special sneak preview!

**When an adorable kitten is abandoned
at the local community center,
Michael and Mia step in to help. . . .**

Michael wasn't sure how to catch a kitten, especially one that didn't seem very friendly. He looked around the room, trying to picture the situation as if it were a basketball play. Sometimes that was a great way to solve problems. "Hey!" he said, pointing to a bunch of foam blocks in a crate.

"Maybe we can use those." He went over and pulled a few out. "He's got himself in a corner," he said to Pete. "What if Mia and I trap him behind the rack with these? The rack is pretty high, so he probably won't try to jump it. Then maybe you can lean over and get him out?"

Pete raised his eyebrows and nodded. "It could work. You'll have to be fast with the blocks, or he'll slip out."

Michael and Mia looked at each other, smiled, and nodded. "We can do it," Michael said.

"Okay, let's give it a try." Pete closed the door to the hallway.

Michael slid the crate of blocks over to where the kitten was hiding. "Ready?" he asked.

"Ready," said Mia.

As fast as they could, Mia and Michael lined up all the blocks so they filled the space under the rack, without a single opening for the kitten to escape through.

"Okay, Pete," Michael said.

Pete came up and peeked over the rack. "Hey, little fella," Pete said softly. "We're just trying to help you." Pete stretched out his arm and bent over the rack. "That's it. Stay right there. Okay. I gotcha." Pete started to straighten up, his hand under the tabby's belly. The kitten's orange-striped legs hung loosely in the air.

"Nice work, guys," Pete said as he pulled the kitten to his chest.

"Good plan, big brother." Mia nudged Michael in the ribs with her elbow. He grinned at her, then stood up and peered at the little kitten cradled in Pete's arms. There was still a little French fry salt on his whiskers. He didn't look fierce at all. He looked adorable.

"Why would anybody leave a little kitten behind like that, stuck in a fast-food bag like he was garbage?" Michael asked. It made him mad. How could people treat animals so badly?

Pete shook his head. "Who knows? Anyway, we rescued the little guy," Pete said. "Now what?"

"We should make sure he's not hurt," Mia suggested.

Pete held up the little tabby cat, both hands just under the kitten's front legs, and looked into his big, yellow eyes. "Are you okay, fella?" The kitten let out a raspy meow, and his little nose quivered. "You look pretty good for having been stuffed into a paper bag. You're much cuter than a hamburger, but you should still see a vet. And get a bath!"

First I was stuck in that bag. Now I'm hanging up in the air! But I feel safe. This guy's hands are strong and warm. His voice is kind and low. I think I can trust him. I hope I can.

Michael laughed. The little kitten's wide-eyed expression was hilarious. It almost looked as if the tabby understood what Pete was saying.

"We could take him to Dr. Bulford at Wags and Whiskers," Mia said. She clasped her hands together and bounced on her tiptoes. "That's where we took Callie."

"Who's Callie?" Pete asked. While Michael told Pete all about Callie, Mia scratched the tabby kitten under his chin.

"We could foster this kitten, too, right?" she said to Michael. "He needs help. He needs a family of his own."

Michael swallowed. He looked from Mia to the tiny tabby to Pete. It was true. The kitten did need a family, but were they the family he needed?

**Look for OTIS, available now,
and find out if this sweet kitten
finds his forever home.**

THE PUPPY PLACE

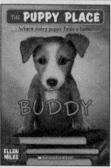

WHERE EVERY PUPPY FINDS A HOME

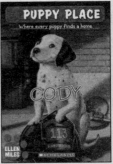

Read them all!

ABOUT THE AUTHOR

ELLEN MILES loves dogs, which is why she has a great time writing The Puppy Place books. And guess what? She loves cats, too! (In fact, her very first pet was a beautiful tortoiseshell cat named Jenny.) That's why she came up with a brand-new series called Kitty Corner. Ellen lives in Vermont and loves to be outdoors every day, walking, biking, skiing, or swimming, depending on the season. She also loves to read, cook, explore her beautiful state, play with dogs, and hang out with friends and family.

Visit Ellen at **www.ellenmiles.net**.